Sweet Dreams: Bedtime Stories for Little Ones

Vaani G

Sweet Dreams: Bedtime stories for Little ones

Kids Kingdom, Volume 1

Vaani G

Published by Vaani G, 2024.

SWEET DREAMS: BEDTIME STORIES FOR LITTLE ONES

First edition. August 9, 2024.

ISBN: 979-8227057198

Written by Vaani G.

DEDICATION

To all the amazing kids out there, this book is dedicated to you. May these stories spark your imagination, take you on exciting adventures, and remind you that the best moments often happen beyond the screen. Keep dreaming, exploring, and believing in the magic within you.

The Sleepy Star

IN A FARAWAY SKY, THERE lived a little star named Twinkle. Twinkle was always sleepy and struggled to shine as brightly as the other stars. One night, Twinkle's friends noticed that she was dimmer than usual. The other stars, seeing her struggle, decided to share a bit of their own light with her. They surrounded Twinkle and together, they shone so brightly that the whole night sky sparkled like never before. Twinkle felt warm and happy, realizing that her friends' kindness made her glow. From that night on, Twinkle always shared her light with other stars who needed it. She learned that sharing not only helps others but also brings joy to the giver.

'Sharing brings joy'

Benny the Brave Bunny

BENNY WAS A SMALL BUNNY who lived in a big, green meadow. One day, he lost his favorite carrot while playing. Benny was scared of the dark and the shadows in the meadow, but he wanted his carrot back. He took a deep breath and hopped bravely into the meadow. Along the way, he met other animals who cheered him on. Benny found his carrot near a big tree. As he hopped back home, he felt proud and brave. He learned that even though he was small, he could be very brave. Benny's bravery inspired his friends, and they all felt a little braver knowing that size doesn't matter when it comes to courage.

'Bravery comes in small packages'

The Kindness Tree

LILY LOVED PLANTING seeds in her garden. One day, she planted a special seed called the Kindness Tree. Her grandmother told her that this tree grows with every kind act she does. Lily started helping her friends, sharing her toys, and being nice to everyone. To her amazement, the Kindness Tree grew taller and fuller each time she did something kind. Soon, the tree was the most beautiful one in the garden. Birds made nests in it, and its shade gave comfort to everyone. Lily realized that her kindness not only made the tree grow but also spread happiness all around. She learned that kindness is like a seed that grows and spreads, making the world a better place.

'Acts of kindness grow and spread'

Timmy's Tidy Room

TIMMY'S ROOM WAS ALWAYS messy, and he could never find his toys. His mom always told him to clean it, but Timmy thought it was too much work. One day, Timmy decided to give it a try. He put his toys in their places, folded his clothes, and made his bed. When he was done, Timmy looked around and felt proud. His room looked bright and spacious. That night, he found his favorite book easily and read it before bed. Timmy felt happy and peaceful. He realized that a tidy room made him feel good and made it easier to find his things. From then on, Timmy kept his room tidy, knowing that a clean space brings happiness and calm.

'Tidiness brings happiness'

The Little Cloud's Big Heart

HIGH UP IN THE SKY, there was a little cloud named Puffy. Puffy loved floating around and watching the world below. One sunny day, Puffy noticed that the flowers in the garden were wilting from the heat. Puffy wanted to help them but didn't know how. Then, Puffy had an idea. She gathered all her rain and floated over the garden, gently sprinkling water on the thirsty flowers. The flowers perked up and looked more beautiful than ever. Puffy felt a warm glow inside her. She learned that generosity comes from the heart and even small acts of kindness can make a big difference. Puffy continued to help the flowers whenever they needed rain, making the garden bloom with her big heart.

'Generosity comes from the heart'

Friends of the Forest

IN THE HEART OF A BIG forest, a group of animals decided to build a playground. Each animal had different skills: the beavers were good at building, the birds could fetch small things, and the deer could carry heavy logs. They all worked together, using their unique abilities to help build the playground. The beavers built the structures, the birds brought twigs and leaves, and the deer carried the heavy parts. Soon, they had a beautiful playground with swings, slides, and a climbing tree. The animals played together happily, knowing that their teamwork made it all possible. They learned that when everyone works together, they can achieve great things and make their dreams come true.

'Teamwork makes dreams work'

Bella's Bedtime Adventure

EVERY NIGHT, BELLA'S mom told her a bedtime before she went to sleep. Bella loved these stories because they took her on magical adventures. One night, Bella imagined herself as a brave knight saving a kingdom from a dragon. Another night, she was a mermaid exploring the deep ocean with her fish friends. Each filled her with excitement and wonder. Bella's dreams were always full of adventures because of the stories. She learned that her imagination could take her anywhere and make any dream come true. Bella's bedtime became her favorite time, where she could explore new worlds and be anything she wanted to be, all thanks to the power of her imagination.

'Imagination is powerful'

The Helpful Hedgehog

HENRY THE HEDGEHOG lived in a cozy burrow in the forest. He loved his home but noticed that some of his friends had problems. The birds needed help building their nests, and the rabbits needed help digging new burrows. Henry decided to help. He used his spiky back to gather twigs for the birds and his strong paws to help the rabbits dig. Everyone was grateful for Henry's help, and they all thanked him warmly. Henry felt a deep sense of happiness from helping his friends. He realized that helping others not only made them happy but also brought joy to his own heart. From then on, Henry continued to help whenever he could, knowing that helping others brings true happiness.

'Helping others brings happiness'

Daisy's Dream Garden

DAISY LOVED FLOWERS and wanted to have the most beautiful garden in the village. She planted seeds and watered them every day. She was excited to see them grow but became impatient when nothing happened after a few days. Daisy's grandmother told her that flowers take time to bloom. Daisy decided to wait patiently. Every day, she watered the seeds and took care of them. One morning, Daisy woke up to find her garden full of colorful flowers. She was overjoyed and proud of her beautiful garden. Daisy learned that patience and care bring beautiful results. Her garden became the talk of the village, and Daisy felt happy knowing that her patience had paid off.

'Patience yields beautiful results'

Max's Magical Blanket

MAX HAD A MAGICAL BLANKET that made him feel safe at night. Whenever he was scared of the dark or heard strange noises, he would wrap himself in his blanket, and all his fears would go away. One night, Max couldn't find his blanket. He felt scared and didn't know what to do. His mom told him that he was brave even without the blanket. Max took a deep breath and faced the dark. To his surprise, he found that he wasn't as scared as he thought. He realized that his courage came from within, not just from the blanket. Max learned that he was strong and brave on his own. From then on, Max felt secure knowing that true courage comes from inside him.

'Security comes from within'

The Lost Little Lamb

LILA THE LAMB GOT LOST while playing in the meadow. She wandered around, feeling scared and alone. Her friends, the other lambs, noticed she was missing and decided to look for her. They called out her name and searched every corner of the meadow. Lila heard their voices and followed the sound. Soon, she saw her friends coming towards her. They hugged her and led her back home. Lila felt safe and happy, knowing that her friends cared for her. She learned that friends are always there to help us find our way when we're lost. Lila appreciated her friends even more and felt grateful for their love and support.

'Friends help us find our way'

Oliver's Ocean Adventure

OLIVER THE OCTOPUS loved exploring the ocean. One day, he found a strange, shiny object on the ocean floor. Curious, he picked it up and examined it. It was a beautiful, glowing pearl. Oliver showed it to his friends, and they were all amazed. They decided to explore the area together and found more hidden treasures and beautiful sea creatures. Oliver's curiosity led them to discover a whole new part of the ocean they had never seen before. Oliver learned that being curious and exploring new things can lead to wonderful discoveries. He continued his adventures, always eager to see what new wonders the ocean had in store.

'Curiosity leads to new discoveries'

The Gentle Giant

IN A SMALL VILLAGE, there was a giant named Greg. Greg was big and strong, but he was also very gentle. He loved helping the villagers with their chores, but he was always careful not to hurt anyone with his big hands. One day, a tiny bird fell out of its nest. Greg gently picked up the bird and put it back in its nest, making sure it was safe. The villagers saw Greg's kindness and realized that his gentleness was a great strength. Greg learned that being gentle and kind is just as important as being strong. From then on, he continued to help the villagers with his gentle touch, and everyone admired and loved him even more.

'Gentleness is a strength'

The Rainbow Butterfly

In a lush garden, there was a butterfly named Bella. Bella had rainbow-colored wings that were different from the other butterflies. At first, Bella felt shy and wished she had plain wings like everyone else. But as she flew around, her colorful wings caught the sunlight and created beautiful patterns. The other butterflies and insects admired Bella's wings and told her how beautiful they were. Bella realized that her unique wings made her special and brought joy to others. She learned that being different is beautiful and something to be proud of. Bella flew happily, spreading her rainbow colors and reminding everyone that diversity makes the world a more beautiful place.

'Diversity is beautiful'

Sam's Silly Socks

Sam loved wearing silly, colorful socks. He had socks with stripes, polka dots, and even ones with funny faces. Some kids at school teased Sam about his socks, but he didn't mind. Sam's socks made him happy and he liked being different. One day, the school had a special event where everyone was asked to wear their silliest socks. Sam's friends realized how much fun it was to wear unique socks, and they all joined in. They laughed and admired each other's socks. Sam learned that embracing what makes you unique can inspire others to do the same. He continued to wear his silly socks proudly, knowing that being different was something to celebrate.

'Embrace what makes you unique'

The Little Red Wagon

An ant named Andy had a little red wagon that he used to carry food back to his nest. One day, Andy found a big piece of fruit that was too heavy for him to pull alone. He struggled and felt tired. His friends saw him and decided to help. The ladybug, the beetle, and the butterfly all pitched in, helping Andy pull the wagon. With everyone's help, they moved the heavy load easily. Andy felt grateful and happy. He learned that with helping hands, even the heaviest loads become lighter. Andy's friends were always there to support him, and he knew that teamwork made everything easier.

'Helping hands make the load lighter'

The Moon's Secret

Every night, the moon shone brightly in the sky, watching over the world. One evening, a little star asked the moon why it shone so brightly. The moon smiled and told the star that everyone has a special light inside them. Some shine brightly like the sun, and others softly like the stars, but all lights are important. The little star felt inspired and began to shine a bit brighter. The moon's words spread among the stars, and soon the night sky was filled with twinkling lights. The little star learned that everyone has a unique light that makes the world brighter. From then on, it shone with pride, knowing its light was special.

'Everyone has a special light'

Peter's Perfect Picnic

Peter planned a perfect picnic in the park. He made sandwiches, packed fruits, and brought his favorite blanket. But when he arrived, things didn't go as planned. The wind blew his napkins away, ants crawled onto his food, and he spilled his juice. Peter felt disappointed and thought his picnic was ruined. But then, his friends started playing games, telling jokes, and laughing. Peter realized that even though things weren't perfect, he was having a great time. He learned that happiness doesn't come from perfection but from enjoying the moment and being with friends. Peter had the best picnic ever, filled with laughter and fun.

'Perfection isn't necessary for happiness'

Lily and the Ladybug

Lily loved playing in her garden. One day, she saw a ladybug struggling to find its way back home. Lily gently picked up the ladybug and placed it on a leaf near its home. The ladybug's family was happy to see it return. Lily felt a warm glow inside her heart. She realized that even small acts of kindness, like helping a tiny ladybug, made a big difference. From that day, Lily made it a habit to help whenever she could, no matter how small the act. She learned that kindness, no matter how small, always matters and makes the world a better place.

'Small acts of kindness matter'

The Whispering Wind

On a breezy day, a group of children played in the meadow. They heard the wind whispering through the trees and decided to listen closely. The wind told them stories about the old oak tree, the river's journey, and the mountains far away. The children were amazed by the stories and felt a deep connection to nature. They learned to listen to the sounds around them and discovered that the world was full of wisdom and wonder. The whispering wind taught them that by being quiet and listening, they could learn and appreciate the beauty of the world. The children continued to listen to the wind, feeling grateful for its gentle guidance.

'Listen to the world around you'

The Little Star and the Big Sky

Once upon a time, in the big, big sky, there was a little star. The star was very small and shy. It thought, "I'm so tiny, no one can see me shine."

One night, the Moon said, "Little Star, why don't you shine bright tonight?"

The Little Star was scared but decided to try. It twinkled and shined with all its might. Suddenly, all the animals on Earth looked up and saw the beautiful Little Star shining brightly.

The animals said, "Wow! Look at that little star! It's so pretty!"

The Little Star was happy and learned that even if you're small, you can still shine bright and make a difference.

'You don't have to be big to shine bright'

VAANI G

The Brave Little Bunny

In a green meadow, there lived a tiny bunny named Harry.
Harry loved to hop around and play. One day, Harry found a
big carrot patch. But there was a problem—there was a big fence
around it!
Harry really wanted a carrot, but he was scared of the fence.
Then, Harry remembered his mom's words, "If you want
something, be brave and try your best."
So, Harry took a deep breath and tried to jump over the fence.
He jumped and jumped, and finally, he made it over! Harry got
his carrot and felt very proud.
'Be brave and try your best, even if things seem hard'

The Helpful Squirrel

Once, in a tall tree, lived a squirrel named Sammy. Sammy loved to collect nuts. One day, a strong wind blew, and all the nuts fell down the hill. Sammy was sad.

His friend, the bird, saw him and asked, "What's wrong, Sammy?"

Sammy said, "The wind blew away all my nuts!"

The bird flew to the other animals and said, "Let's help Sammy!"

The animals came together and brought back all the nuts.

Sammy was very happy and thanked everyone.

'Friends help each other'

VAANI G

The Curious Caterpillar

In a garden, there was a little caterpillar named Coco. Coco loved to explore and see new things. One day, Coco saw a butterfly and thought, "Wow, I want to fly like that!"
Coco asked the butterfly, "How do I become like you?"
The butterfly smiled and said, "You have to be patient and wait. One day, you'll turn into a butterfly too!"
Coco was excited and waited patiently. After some time, Coco became a beautiful butterfly and flew around the garden.
'Be patient, good things come with time'

The Sharing Bear

In a big forest, there was a bear named Joe. Joe loved honey. One day, he found a big pot of honey. He was so happy that he didn't want to share with anyone.

But then, he saw his friend the deer, looking sad. The deer hadn't eaten all day. Joe remembered his mom's words, "It's nice to share."

So, Joe called his friend and shared the honey with him. They both ate and were happy together.

'Sharing is caring'

The Colorful Crayons

In a little box, there lived a bunch of crayons. Each crayon had a different color. Red crayon thought it was the best because it was bright and bold. Blue crayon thought it was the best because it was calm and cool. They all argued about who was the best.

One day, a little boy picked up the box of crayons and drew a beautiful picture with all the colors. The crayons saw that when they worked together, they could make something beautiful.

'Working together makes things better'

The Lost Little Duckling

In a big pond, there lived a family of ducks. The smallest
duckling, Ducky, loved to explore. One day, Ducky wandered
too far and got lost. Ducky was scared and started to cry.
A kind fish swam by and asked, "What's wrong, little duckling?"
Ducky said, "I can't find my way home!"
The fish said, "Don't worry, I'll help you!" The fish guided
Ducky back to the pond. Ducky was happy to be home and
learned to stay close to the family.

'It's important to stay close to those who care about you'

The Sleepy Owl

In a tall tree, there lived a sleepy owl named Ollie. Ollie loved to sleep during the day and stay awake at night. But one day, Ollie couldn't sleep because the tree was too noisy.

Ollie asked the woodpecker, "Can you stop pecking? I can't sleep!"

The woodpecker said, "I'm sorry, Ollie. I need to peck to find food."

Ollie understood and decided to fly to a quieter tree. Ollie learned that sometimes, it's okay to move to a better place if the old place isn't working.

'Sometimes it's okay to make a change if it helps you feel better'

The Kind Little Ant

In a big anthill, there lived a little ant named Andy. Andy was very kind and always helped others. One day, Andy saw a ladybug struggling to climb a leaf.
Andy went up to the ladybug and said, "Do you need help?"
The ladybug smiled and said, "Yes, please!"
Andy helped the ladybug climb the leaf. The ladybug was so happy and thanked Andy. Later, when Andy needed help carrying a big crumb, the ladybug came to help.
'When you're kind, kindness comes back to you'

The Clever Little Mouse

In a cozy little hole lived a clever mouse named Mickey. One day, Mickey found a big piece of cheese. But there was a cat nearby, watching the cheese.

Mickey thought, "How can I get the cheese without the cat catching me?"

Mickey had an idea. He found a small stick and poked the cheese from a distance. The cheese rolled away, and the cat got distracted. Mickey quickly grabbed the cheese and ran back to his hole.

'Look for ways to come out of tough situations'

The Friendly Firefly

In a dark forest, there lived a little firefly named Flicker. Flicker loved to fly around and light up the night. One night, Flicker noticed that a group of animals was scared because it was so dark.

Flicker flew over to the animals and said, "Don't be scared! I'll light the way for you."

Flicker led the way, and the animals followed. They felt safe with Flicker's light. The animals thanked Flicker for being so kind and helpful.

'Helping others can make them feel safe and happy'

The Turtle and the Snail

Tina the Turtle and Sammy the Snail were best friends. They both loved to explore the garden, but they were very slow. One day, they saw a rabbit hopping quickly by and felt sad that they couldn't move as fast.

Tina said, "I wish we could be fast like the rabbit."

Sammy smiled and said, "We may be slow, but we always enjoy the journey and see many beautiful things."

They continued their slow journey, noticing the pretty flowers and the warm sunshine. They realized that going slow helped them appreciate the little things.

'Sometimes it's good to take things slow and enjoy the journey'

The Honest Little Dog

In a small village, there was a little dog named Max. Max loved to play with his ball. One day, while playing, he accidentally broke a vase in his owner's house. Max felt bad and didn't know what to do.

Max thought about hiding, but then he remembered that honesty is the best policy. He went to his owner and barked, showing the broken vase.

His owner said, "Thank you for telling me the truth, Max. I'm glad you're honest."

Max felt good about being honest and learned that telling the truth is always the best choice.

'Always tell the truth, even if it's hard'

The Wise Old Tree

In a peaceful meadow, there stood a wise old tree. All the animals loved to come and talk to the tree because it gave good advice. One day, a young bird came to the tree and said, "I'm scared to fly. What if I fall?"

The wise old tree said, "Little bird, you may fall, but that's okay. Everyone falls sometimes. But if you don't try, you'll never know how high you can fly."

The little bird took the tree's advice and bravely tried to fly. It flapped its wings and, after a few tries, soared high in the sky.

The bird was happy and thanked the tree.

'It's okay to be afraid, but trying new things can help you grow'

VAANI G

The Generous Little Elephant

Ellie the Elephant loved to collect flowers. She had a beautiful garden full of colorful blooms. One day, a group of bees came to her and said, "Ellie, we're hungry and need flowers for nectar." Ellie looked at her garden and thought, "I have so many flowers. I can share with the bees."
Ellie gave the bees some flowers, and they were very grateful. Later, the bees brought Ellie some sweet honey as a thank-you gift. Ellie was happy to help.
'Being generous makes you a good person'

The Brave Little Seed

In a big garden, there was a tiny seed. The seed was buried deep in the ground and felt scared. "How will I grow?" it wondered. But the seed decided to be brave and began to push through the soil.

Days went by, and the seed sprouted into a small plant. It faced many challenges: heavy rain, strong winds, and even some pesky bugs. But the plant kept growing, believing in itself. Soon, it blossomed into a beautiful sunflower, tall and proud.

The other plants admired the sunflower and said, "You were just a tiny seed, but now you're the tallest flower in the garden!"

The sunflower smiled and said, "I never gave up, even when things were tough."

'Be brave and persistent, and you can overcome challenges'

VAANI G

The Magic Paintbrush

Once upon a time, there was a girl named Lily who loved to paint. She wasn't very rich, but she was happy with her little brushes and colors. One day, she found a shiny paintbrush lying in the grass. She picked it up and decided to paint with it.
To her surprise, whatever she painted came to life! She painted a loaf of bread, and it appeared right in front of her. Lily was amazed and started painting things her village needed—food for the hungry, clothes for the poor, and toys for the children. However, a greedy man in the village heard about the magic brush and wanted it for himself. He tried to take it from Lily, but she refused, saying, "This brush is for helping others, not for greed."
The greedy man didn't listen and tried to use the brush, but it wouldn't work for him. Realizing his mistake, he apologized, and Lily continued using the brush to help her village.
'Use your talents and gifts to help others, not for selfish reasons'

The Lost Treasure of Kindness

A long time ago, in a small town, there was a legend about a hidden treasure. The legend said that only a kind heart could find it. Many people searched for it, but no one found it.

One day, a young boy named Tom decided to look for the treasure. As he walked through the town, he saw an old man struggling to carry his bags. Tom helped the old man, who smiled and thanked him. Further along, Tom saw a child crying because she lost her puppy. He helped her find it, and she was very happy.

Tom continued to help everyone he met without thinking about the treasure. At the end of the day, as he walked back home, he found a small box on his doorstep. Inside, there was a note that read, "The greatest treasure is kindness."

Tom realized that by being kind and helping others, he had found the real treasure.

'Kindness is the greatest treasure of all'

The Tale of the Whispering Willow

In a quiet village, there was a magical tree called the Whispering Willow. The villagers believed that the tree could grant wishes if you whispered your wish into its leaves. Many people came to the tree, wishing for wealth, fame, and fortune.

One day, a poor girl named Mia came to the tree. She whispered, "I wish for everyone to be happy and have enough to eat." The tree's leaves rustled, and suddenly, the village started to flourish. Crops grew abundantly, and everyone had enough food.

The villagers were amazed and happy. They realized that Mia's selfless wish had made everyone's lives better. They thanked Mia and learned the importance of thinking about others.

'Selflessness and thinking of others can bring joy and prosperity to everyone'

The Clever Crow and the Tricky Fox

In a dense forest, there lived a clever crow named Corbin. He was known for his sharp mind. One day, while flying, Corbin found a piece of bread and took it to a tree to eat. A hungry fox saw this and thought of a plan to get the bread.

The fox approached the tree and said, "Oh, Corbin, you have such a beautiful voice! Would you sing a song for me?"

Corbin knew the fox was trying to trick him, but he decided to play along. He pretended to clear his throat and dropped the bread, but not onto the ground. Instead, he quickly caught it in his beak again.

The fox was surprised and asked, "Why didn't you drop the bread?"

Corbin replied, "I know your tricks, Mr. Fox. You can't fool me that easily."

The fox realized that he couldn't outsmart Corbin and walked away, hungry and disappointed.

'Be aware of trickery and think before you act'

The Lion's Share

In the jungle, the lion, the king of beasts, declared a grand feast for all the animals. Everyone was excited and brought delicious food. When it was time to share the food, the lion took the biggest portion for himself, leaving little for the others.
The wise old owl noticed this and said, "King Lion, being a leader means sharing fairly with everyone."
The lion thought about it and realized his mistake. He apologized and shared the food equally among all the animals. From that day on, the lion learned the importance of fairness and generosity.
'True leadership means being fair and considerate to everyone'

The Three Little Pigs and the Big Bad Wolf

Three little pigs decided to build houses for themselves. The first pig built his house out of straw, the second pig built his house out of sticks, and the third pig built his house out of bricks. One day, a big bad wolf came and blew down the straw house and the stick house, but he couldn't blow down the brick house. The two pigs who had lost their homes ran to their brother's brick house, where they were safe from the wolf. The three pigs learned that hard work and planning are important, as the third pig's brick house protected them all.
'Hard work and careful planning pay off'

The Little Blue Bird's Song

In a colorful forest, there lived a little blue bird who loved to sing. However, the other animals thought her voice was strange and made fun of her. Feeling sad, the blue bird stopped singing and hid in a tree.

One day, the forest was covered in a thick fog, and the animals couldn't find their way home. The little blue bird realized she could help and started singing her unique song. The animals followed the sound and found their way back home safely. The animals apologized for making fun of her, and they all agreed that her song was beautiful and special.

'Everyone has something unique and valuable to offer'

The Tale of the Lost Book

In a small town, there was a library filled with wonderful books. A young boy named Alex loved to read. One day, he borrowed a book but lost it on his way home. He was worried and searched everywhere but couldn't find it.

Alex went back to the library and confessed to the librarian. The librarian smiled and said, "It's okay, Alex. The important thing is that you were honest."

Later, a kind neighbor found the book and returned it to the library. Alex was relieved and learned the importance of honesty and taking responsibility.

'Honesty is the best policy, and taking responsibility is important'

The Rabbit and the Turtle's Race

The rabbit was very proud of how fast he could run. He often bragged to the other animals and made fun of the slow turtle.
One day, the turtle challenged the rabbit to a race.
The rabbit laughed and agreed, thinking he would win easily.
During the race, the rabbit ran quickly but decided to take a nap, thinking he had plenty of time. The turtle, slow but steady, kept moving without stopping.
When the rabbit woke up, he saw that the turtle was near the finish line. He ran as fast as he could, but the turtle crossed the finish line first and won the race.

'Slow and steady wins the race'

The Little Lighthouse

On a rocky shore stood a little lighthouse. It was small but had a bright light that guided ships safely to shore. The lighthouse keeper took great care of it, making sure the light never went out.

One stormy night, a ship was struggling in the rough waters. The little lighthouse shone its light brightly, helping the ship's captain see the rocks and avoid danger. The ship safely reached the harbor, thanks to the little lighthouse.

The lighthouse keeper smiled, knowing that even small things can have a big impact.

'Even small acts of kindness and help can make a big difference'

The Clever Spider and the Greedy Fly

A clever spider spun a beautiful web in the corner of a house. A fly saw the web and thought, "This web looks nice, but it's dangerous. I should stay away."
But then the spider called out, "Dear fly, come and see the beautiful web I've made. You can rest here if you're tired."
The fly hesitated, but the web looked so inviting. As the fly flew closer, the spider caught it. The fly realized too late that it should have trusted its instincts.
'Be cautious and don't be easily swayed by appearances'

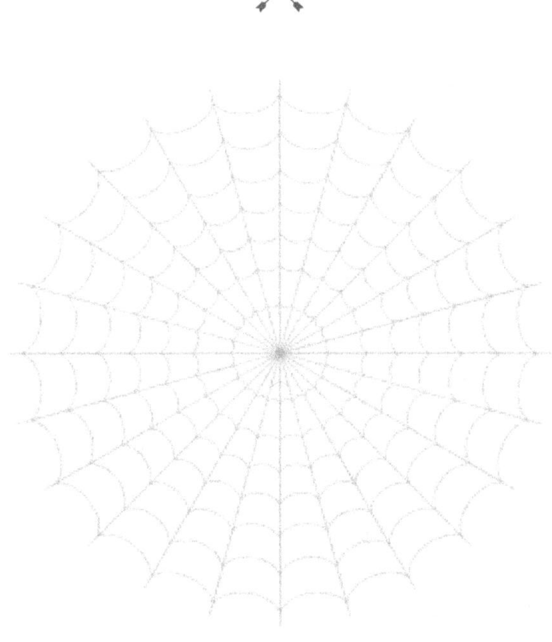

VAANI G

The Lion and the Mouse

One day, a lion caught a little mouse. The mouse pleaded for its life, promising to help the lion someday. The lion laughed but let the mouse go.

A few days later, the lion got caught in a hunter's net. The mouse heard the lion's roars and came to help. It nibbled through the ropes and freed the lion. The lion was grateful and learned that even the smallest creatures can be helpful.

'No act of kindness is ever wasted'

The Curious Cat and the Mysterious Box

In a small village, there was a curious cat named Whiskers. One day, Whiskers found a mysterious box with a note that read, "Do not open." Whiskers was very curious and wanted to know what was inside.

Despite the warning, Whiskers opened the box and found a beautiful butterfly trapped inside. The butterfly flew out, grateful for its freedom. It told Whiskers, "Thank you for freeing me, but remember, curiosity can sometimes lead to trouble."

Whiskers learned that while curiosity is natural, it's important to respect warnings and be careful.

'It's good to be curious, but always be cautious and respect boundaries'

The Golden Touch

King Midas was obsessed with gold and wished that everything he touched would turn to gold. His wish was granted, and at first, he was thrilled. He touched furniture, flowers, and even his meals, transforming everything into gold. However, he soon faced problems: his food turned to gold, and he could no longer eat. When he hugged his beloved daughter, she turned into a solid gold statue.

Desperate and heartbroken, Midas begged to have his wish undone. He realized that his greed had turned his life into a gilded cage. He longed for the simple joys he had taken for granted—warm food and loving embraces. His wish was granted once more, and he learned to appreciate the true value of life's simple pleasures.

'Greed can lead to unhappiness, and the simple joys in life are often the most valuable'

The Peacock's Complaint

A proud peacock admired his magnificent feathers but envied the nightingale's enchanting song. He complained to the goddess Juno about how the nightingale's voice was far more charming than his own appearance. Juno listened patiently and then gently explained that every creature has its own unique gifts and beauty.

She told the peacock that while his feathers were extraordinary, the nightingale's voice was equally special in its own way. Realizing that each gift has its own value, the peacock began to appreciate his own stunning feathers. He understood that he didn't need to envy others to value himself.

'Appreciate your own unique qualities and talents'

The Starfish Thrower

One morning, a boy walked along the beach, picking up stranded starfish and tossing them back into the sea. A man saw him and said, "There are too many starfish. You can't make a difference."

Undeterred, the boy picked up another starfish, threw it into the water, and replied, "It made a difference to that one." Despite the man's doubts, the boy continued his task, knowing that each small action mattered. His simple act of kindness saved countless starfish, showing that even the smallest efforts can have a significant impact.

'Small actions can make a big difference'

The Mouse and the Elephant

Once, a mouse saw an elephant in distress with a thorn stuck in his foot. Despite the size difference, the mouse bravely helped remove the thorn. The grateful elephant thanked the mouse and promised to return the favor if needed.

Some time later, the mouse was caught by a hungry cat. Hearing the mouse's cries, the elephant remembered his promise. He arrived just in time, using his trunk to lift the cat away and rescue the mouse.

The mouse was overjoyed and thanked the elephant, realizing that even the smallest acts of kindness can lead to great friendships and help.

'No act of kindness is too small, and friends come in all sizes'

The Shepherd and the Wolf

A dedicated shepherd tended his flock with great care, ensuring they were always safe and well-fed. One evening, as dusk fell, he noticed a shadowy figure lurking near his sheep. It was a wolf, waiting for the perfect moment to strike. The shepherd, sensing the danger, bravely confronted the wolf and chased it away with loud shouts and a sturdy stick.

The next morning, the shepherd's flock gathered around him, expressing their gratitude. They bleated in appreciation, recognizing how his vigilance had kept them safe through the night. The shepherd felt a deep sense of pride and fulfillment, knowing his efforts were valued.

As he continued his work, the shepherd reflected on the previous night's events. He understood that his diligence and constant watchfulness were crucial in protecting his flock. His hard work had not gone unnoticed, and the safety of his sheep was a testament to his dedication.

The shepherd's commitment and careful attention had made a significant difference, reinforcing the importance of being vigilant and diligent in every task.

'Diligence and vigilance are important virtues that ensure safety and success'

The Eagle and the Tortoise

A tortoise admired the soaring eagles and wished he could fly like them. He approached an eagle and asked for help to experience the skies. The eagle, being kind-hearted, agreed to carry the tortoise up into the air.

As they ascended, the tortoise looked down and felt a surge of fear. The vastness of the sky and the ground far below made him anxious. Despite the eagle's gentle reassurances, the tortoise's fear grew. He asked the eagle to bring him back down.

The eagle gracefully descended, placing the tortoise back on solid ground. Once back, the tortoise realized he felt most comfortable where he belonged. He understood that his true happiness came from being himself, on the ground, where he could live his life contentedly.

The tortoise thanked the eagle and was grateful for the experience, embracing his own unique place in the world.

'Be content with who you are and find happiness in your own abilities'

The Mice and the Bell

The mice in a house were terrorized by a cat. They held a meeting to find a solution. One mouse suggested putting a bell on the cat to hear it coming. Everyone agreed it was a great idea until one mouse asked, "Who will bell the cat?" They realized it's easy to propose solutions but difficult to implement them.

'Practical solutions are more important than just ideas'

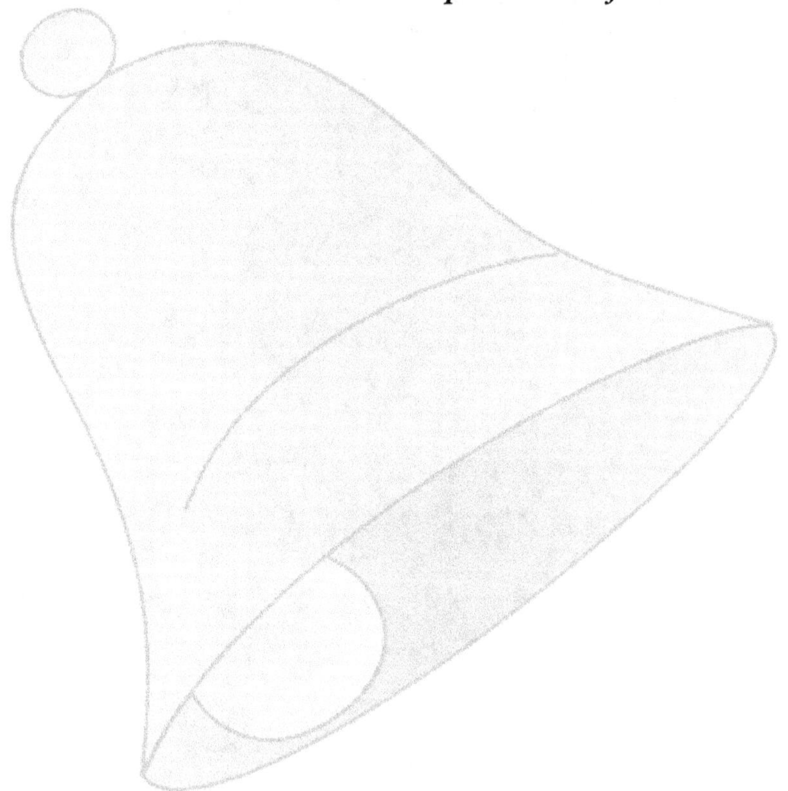

The Brave Little Ant

One sunny day, a little ant discovered a large piece of bread. It was far bigger than himself, but the ant was determined to move it to his colony. He pushed and pulled with all his might, but the bread wouldn't budge. Undeterred, the brave little ant called upon his fellow ants for help.

Together, the ants formed a line and worked as a team. They coordinated their efforts, each ant contributing its strength. Slowly but surely, they moved the bread inch by inch. The journey was long and challenging, but the ants didn't give up. They encouraged one another and stayed focused on their goal. After much hard work and determination, the ants finally brought the bread to their colony. Their combined efforts ensured they had enough food to last through the entire winter. The colony celebrated their achievement, proud of what they had accomplished together.

'Teamwork and determination can accomplish great things'

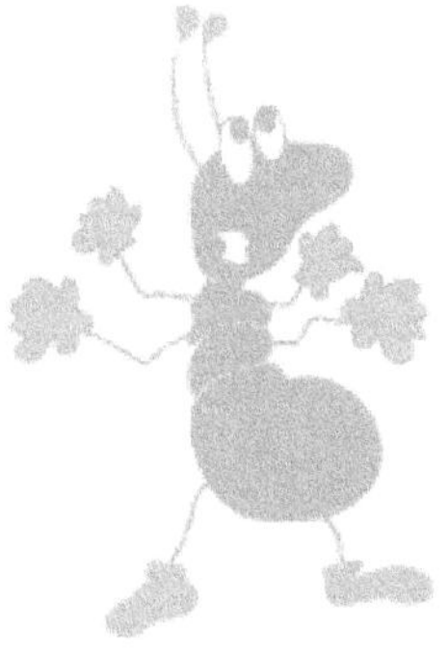

The Frog and the Well

A frog lived in a well, believing it was the whole world. One day, another frog who had seen the ocean told him about the vast sea. The well frog refused to believe there was a world beyond his well. However, the ocean frog's stories of the wide, beautiful ocean eventually convinced him to leap out and see for himself. When he saw the vast world beyond the well, the well frog was amazed and grateful for the ocean frog's persistence. ***'Be open to new ideas and perspectives'***

The Generous Tree

A young boy loved to play around a tree. The tree gave him apples, branches to swing on, and shade to rest. As the boy grew older, he needed more. The tree gave him wood to build a house, and later, its trunk to make a boat. Each time, the tree joyfully gave everything it had to make the boy happy.
In the end, the tree was just a stump. When the boy, now an old man, returned, the tree apologized for having nothing left to give. The boy sat on the stump, now grateful for the tree's lifelong generosity.
'True love is selfless and giving'

The Little Red Hen

A little red hen found some wheat seeds and asked her friends—a cat, a dog, and a duck—to help plant them. They all refused, so she planted the seeds herself. When the wheat was ready, she asked for help to harvest it, but again they refused. She asked for help to mill the wheat and bake the bread, but they refused each time.

Finally, the little red hen baked the bread herself. When it was ready, her friends wanted to eat it, but she said, "I did all the work, so I will eat the bread myself."

'Hard work and cooperation are valuable and rewarding'

The Friendly Dragon

In a village, there was a dragon who was friendly but misunderstood by the villagers, who feared him. A brave girl named Lily decided to befriend the dragon. She discovered that the dragon was kind and gentle, not the monster everyone imagined.

Lily brought the villagers to meet the dragon, showing them his true nature. Slowly, the villagers realized the dragon meant no harm. They welcomed him into their community, and the dragon used his abilities to help the villagers.

'Don't judge others without getting to know them first'

The Magic Porridge Pot

Once, a poor girl received a magic pot that cooked porridge whenever she said, "Cook, little pot, cook." To stop it, she had to say, "Stop, little pot, stop." One day, her mother used the pot but didn't know how to stop it. The porridge overflowed, threatening to flood the village.

The girl returned just in time and shouted, "Stop, little pot, stop." The pot ceased cooking, and the village was saved. The girl shared the porridge with everyone, ensuring no one went hungry.

'With great power comes great responsibility and the importance of sharing'

The Kind-Hearted Fox

Once, a fox found a crow with a broken wing. Instead of hunting the injured bird, the kind-hearted fox took care of it, providing food and shelter until the crow's wing healed. Grateful for the fox's compassion, the crow promised to return the favor.

During a harsh winter, food became scarce. Remembering the fox's kindness, the crow flew out and found food, bringing it back to the hungry fox. The fox was thankful for the crow's help, and they became lifelong friends.

'Kindness and compassion often come back to us when we need them the most'

The Boy Who Cried Wolf

Once upon a time, a shepherd boy tended his flock near a village. Bored and craving attention, he decided to play a prank. "Wolf! Wolf!" he cried, and the villagers rushed to his aid, only to find no wolf. The boy laughed at their expense. He repeated this trick several times, and each time the villagers came running, only to be fooled.

One day, a real wolf appeared and threatened his sheep. Terrified, the boy shouted, "Wolf! Wolf!" But the villagers, tired of his false alarms, ignored his cries. The wolf attacked the flock, and many sheep were lost.

The boy learned a harsh lesson that day: lying had led to distrust, and when he truly needed help, no one believed him. Realizing the gravity of his actions, he regretted his dishonesty and vowed never to lie again.

'Always tell the truth, as dishonesty can have serious consequences'

The Ugly Duckling

A duckling was born looking different from his siblings. Unlike them, his feathers were dull and gray, making him stand out. The other animals teased him, calling him ugly and making him feel unwelcome. Saddened by their harsh words, the duckling decided to leave the farm and wandered away, hoping to find a place where he belonged.

He spent a lonely and harsh winter by himself, enduring the cold and the isolation. As spring arrived, the duckling wandered to a pond and saw his reflection in the water. To his amazement, he had transformed into a beautiful swan. His once dull feathers were now pristine and white, shimmering in the sunlight. The animals who once teased him were in awe of his beauty, but the swan, remembering his past, understood that true beauty takes time to shine. He realized that everyone has their own unique beauty, which may not be apparent at first.

'Everyone has their own unique beauty, which may take time to shine'

The Wise Rabbit and the Foolish Lion

In a forest, a mighty lion ruled with fear, terrorizing all the animals. The lion demanded that the animals bring him food daily, or he would hunt them down. The animals lived in constant fear until a cunning rabbit decided to put an end to the lion's tyranny.

One day, when it was the rabbit's turn to be the lion's meal, he came up with a clever plan. The rabbit approached the lion and told him that another lion had claimed the forest as his own. Furious, the lion demanded to be taken to this rival.

The wise rabbit led the lion to a deep well and pointed inside. The lion looked down and saw his reflection in the water, mistaking it for another lion. Enraged, the lion leaped into the well to attack his supposed rival, only to drown.

With the lion gone, the forest was peaceful once again, and the animals rejoiced, grateful to the clever rabbit.

'Intelligence can overcome brute strength'

The Ant and the Grasshopper

All summer long, a diligent ant worked tirelessly, gathering food for the upcoming winter. He stored grains and seeds, knowing that the cold months would make finding food difficult. Meanwhile, a carefree grasshopper spent his days playing, singing, and enjoying the warm weather. He laughed at the ant for working so hard and didn't think about the future.

As summer ended and winter approached, the grasshopper found himself without any food. The once plentiful fields were now barren, and the cold winds made it impossible to find anything to eat. Desperate and hungry, the grasshopper went to the ant and asked for food.

The ant, though aware of the grasshopper's laziness, took pity on him. He shared his food but also offered a valuable lesson: "During the good times, we must work hard and prepare for the future. Otherwise, we may find ourselves in need when the hard times come."

The grasshopper realized his mistake and promised to work hard and prepare in the future.

'Prepare for the future and work hard'

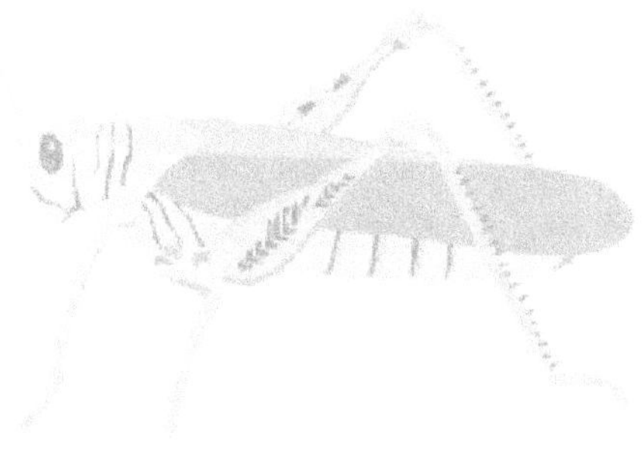

The Honest Woodcutter

A poor woodcutter was chopping wood by a river when, suddenly, his axe slipped from his hands and fell into the deep water. Distressed, he sat by the riverbank, lamenting his loss, as the axe was his only means of livelihood.

Just then, a fairy appeared and asked why he was so upset. The woodcutter explained what had happened, and the fairy, moved by his honesty, decided to help. She dove into the river and emerged with a shiny golden axe. "Is this your axe?" she asked. The woodcutter shook his head and replied, "No, that's not my axe."

The fairy then went back into the water and returned with a silver axe. "Is this your axe?" she asked again.

Once more, the woodcutter replied, "No, that's not my axe either."

Finally, the fairy brought up the woodcutter's old iron axe. The woodcutter smiled and said, "Yes, that's my axe!"

Impressed by his honesty, the fairy rewarded him by giving him all three axes—the golden, the silver, and his own. The woodcutter returned home, grateful and overjoyed, realizing that his honesty had brought him an unexpected reward.

'Honesty is always rewarded'

The Adventure of Timmy the Turtle

Timmy the Turtle was known for his adventurous spirit. While most turtles preferred staying close to their pond, Timmy loved exploring the world around him. One sunny day, as he wandered through the forest, he stumbled upon a hidden path covered in leaves and vines. Curious, Timmy decided to follow it, wondering where it might lead.

The path wound through the trees, and after a while, Timmy emerged into a clearing he had never seen before. In the middle of the clearing was a beautiful, secret pond, surrounded by colorful flowers and tall, shady trees. The water was crystal clear, and it sparkled in the sunlight.

Excited by his discovery, Timmy quickly returned to the pond where his friends lived. He told them all about the secret pond and invited them to come see it. Intrigued, his friends followed Timmy down the hidden path.

When they arrived, they were amazed by the beauty of the secret pond. The turtles splashed in the water, played among the flowers, and enjoyed the peaceful surroundings. They thanked Timmy for his adventurous spirit, grateful that he had shared this wonderful place with them.

'Exploring new places can lead to wonderful discoveries'

VAANI G

ABOUT THE AUTHOR

VAANI G IS A DEDICATED children's author passionate about creating engaging and imaginative stories that captivate young minds while promoting healthier lifestyles. Specializing in kids' categories, her main intention is to reduce screen time by offering captivating alternatives through her vibrant telling and creative narratives. Vaani's works are designed to inspire curiosity, encourage outdoor activities, and foster a love for reading, helping children explore the world beyond screens.

I WOULD LIKE TO EXTEND my heartfelt thanks to everyone who has supported and encouraged me on this journey. To my young readers, your curiosity and enthusiasm inspire every word I write. To the parents and guardians who believe in the power of stories, thank you for fostering a love for reading in your children. And to my family and friends, your unwavering support and love make all things possible. Thank you for being a part of this adventure.

Vaani G